RUFUS LOSES HIS CAPE

A BOOK ABOUT ASKING FOR HELP

By Lucy Bell

Illustrated by Michael Garton

Written by Lucy Bell
Designed by Tim Palin Creative
Illustrated by Michael Garton

Library of Congress Cataloging-in-Publication Data

Names: Bell, Lucy J., author. | Garton, Michael, illustrator.
Title: Rufus loses his cape / by Lucy Bell ; illustrated by Michael Garton.
Description: First edition. | Minneapolis, MN : Sparkhouse Family, 2017. |
    Summary: After a day of imaginary adventures with his cape, Rufus the dog
    loses his "most favorite special something," rejects his animal friends'
    help, and then asks God for forgiveness.
Identifiers: LCCN 2016032667 (print) | LCCN 2016043047 (ebook) | ISBN
    9781506417882 (hardcover : alk. paper) | ISBN 9781506422428 (ebook)
Subjects: | CYAC: Lost and found possessions--Fiction. |
    Imagination--Fiction. | Friendship--Fiction. | Christian life--Fiction.
Classification: LCC PZ7.1.B4523 Ru 2017 (print) | LCC PZ7.1.B4523 (ebook) |
    DDC [E]--dc23
LC record available at https://lccn.loc.gov/2016032667

The paper used in this publication meets the minimum requirements of the American National Standard
for Information Sciences—Permanence of Paper for Printed Library Materials, ANSI Z329.48-1984.

First edition published 2017
Printed in China
22 21 20 19 18 17   2 3 4 5 6 7 8

VN0003466; 9781506417882; NOV2017

SPARK
HOUSE
FAMILY
sparkhousefamily.org

Rufus was very proud of his cape.
He wore it everywhere. It made
him feel strong and important.

His cape was also warm and soft.
When he felt sad, he curled up
in it and snuggled in. It always
made him feel better.

Rufus also liked to use his cape for make-believe.

One day, Rufus was pretending to be a mighty leader.

He announced his presence by playing his horn at the big rock. His cape billowed out behind him.

Rufus marched to the stream. He waved his cape like a flag to welcome incoming ships.

In the meadow, he ate a royal picnic. His cape made a perfect blanket.

It seemed like the fun would never end. It was a great day!

Rufus yawned. All this fun was making him
sleepy. He found a soft patch of grass under a
tree, turned around three times, then curled up.
He reached to pull his cape closer around him.

But it wasn't there! Rufus sat up and looked around. His cape was gone!

Rufus was frantic. His most favorite special something was lost! It could be anywhere!

The more Rufus thought about it, the more worried he became. A big lump the size of a lemon grew in his throat. Tears started to boil behind his eyes. He walked in circles, trying to figure out what to do.

Suddenly he looked up to see his friends coming over. He looked so sad they could tell something was wrong.

"What happened, Rufus?" asked Hal.

"My cape is lost," Rufus sniffed.

"Have you tried walking back to all the places you've been today? That might help you find it," Hal suggested.

But Rufus didn't want Hal's help. He was too sad and too mad. "What a silly idea!" he snapped.

"Ask Uri to help you look," said Ava.
"She can fly up high and see everything."

Uri nodded.

Rufus didn't want Ava or Uri's help either.
He was too upset.

"No. I can do it myself," he muttered.

"Just find something else to do," suggested Jo.
"Maybe you'll find it by accident!"

Rufus snorted and stomped off.

Rufus sniffed the breeze. He couldn't even catch a hint of the smell of his cape he loved so much. Would he *ever* find it?

Rufus's ears drooped. He returned to the soft spot of grass under the tree. He shivered and sniffed.

Today was perfect, he thought.
How did it go wrong?

Rufus curled up into a miserable little ball and thought about his friends. They wanted to help him. He was sorry for not letting them help him look.

Rufus took a deep breath, then
closed his eyes to pray.

*Dear God, I feel so sad and frustrated. Thank you
for friends who want to help me. Amen.*

Rufus opened his eyes. He felt a little better.
Then he went to find his friends.

"Did you find your cape yet?" Ava asked hopefully.

"No," said Rufus. "Will you help me look? I'm sorry I didn't listen before."

Ava grinned. "We forgive you."

Hal asked Rufus to tell them all the places he'd been during the day. Rufus smiled and talked about his adventures.

"I was a brave leader, bringing peace to all the land," Rufus explained.

"I welcomed great ships and ate a royal feast. It was quite a day!" he continued.

"Then lead us, oh brave Rufus!" said Hal.

The friends laughed as Rufus blew his horn and led his friends on a search for his lost cape.

So they raced to the big rock where Rufus had played his horn.

They hurried to the stream and looked in the reeds.

They spread out across the meadow,
searching through the flowers and tall grasses.

Uri flew up high in the sky to see what
she could see.

Rufus was still sad that his cape was lost, but he was happy that his friends cared enough to help him look.

Suddenly, Uri called out from the top of a tall tree. Rufus looked up.

There was his cape, fluttering in the wind! It must have blown away when he tried to take a nap!

Rufus laughed and danced around in a circle. His cape was found, all thanks to his friends!

ABOUT THE STORY

A fun day turns into a nightmare when Rufus's favorite cape goes missing. A prayer about letting friends help reminds Rufus he doesn't have to solve his problems by himself.

DELIGHT IN READING TOGETHER

When reading this story together, act out Rufus's imaginative play with gestures and facial expressions. Use your face and your voice to convey Rufus's disappointment and panic when he loses his cape. Have fun being dramatic.

DEVELOPMENT CONNECTION

Losing a special object, like a blankie or stuffed animal, can be devastating for young children. Use this story as a teaching moment to help your child stay calm the next time something goes missing. It can also be a way to show them how to accept help when they're feeling stubborn or frustrated.

FAITH CONNECTION

The Bible is full of stories of people or things being lost and then found again. God is on mission to save what is lost! That includes us. We can come to God in prayer when we need God's help.

Ask and it will be given to you; seek and you will find; knock and the door will be opened to you. For everyone who asks receives; the one who seeks finds; and to the one who knocks, the door will be opened.

Matthew 7:7-8

SAY A PRAYER

Share this prayer Rufus said when his cape was lost and he didn't know what to do:

Dear God, I feel so sad and frustrated. Thank you for friends who want to help me.

Amen.